# 祖母的星期六湯

# Grandma's Saturday Soup

Written by Sally Fraser

ustrated by Derek Brazell

tonese translation by Sylvia Denham

星期一早上，媽媽很早便叫醒我。
「咪咪，起床，穿衣服上學。」
我睡眼疲睏的爬下床，將窗簾拉開。

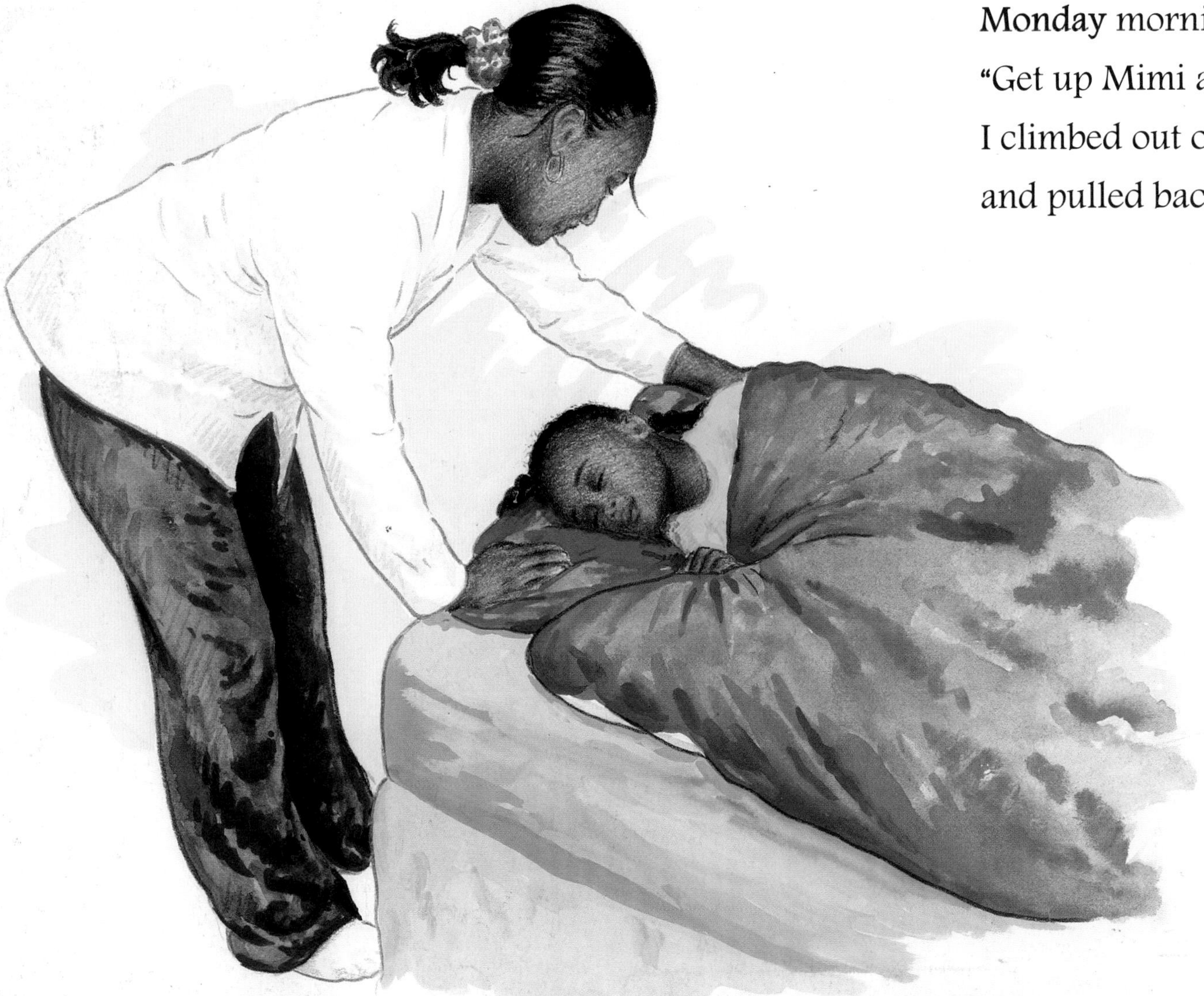

**Monday** morning Mum woke me early.
"Get up Mimi and get dressed for school."
I climbed out of bed all sleepy and tired,
and pulled back the curtains.

早上密雲和寒冷，
天上的雲是白色和鬆軟的，
它們令我想起祖母的星期六湯的湯團。

The morning was cloudy and cold.
The clouds in the sky were white and fluffy.
They reminded me of the dumplings in Grandma's Saturday Soup.

*當我去祖母的家時，她講有關牙買加的故事給我聽。*

*Grandma tells me stories about Jamaica when I go to her house.*

「牙買加的雲會帶來豪雨，
好像有人在天空開了水喉一樣，
溫和的清風將它們吹送，太陽又再次出來了。」

*"The clouds in Jamaica bring the heaviest rain.*
*It's like someone has turned the tap on in the sky.*
*The warm breeze moves them on and the sun comes out again."*

星期二早上，爸爸帶我上學。
這天很寒冷和清新，昨晚曾下過雪。

**Tuesday** morning Dad took me to school.

The day was cold and crisp; it had snowed in the night.

它是白色和柔滑的，很似切開了的甘薯裏面一樣，
就好像祖母的星期六湯的甘薯。

It's white and smooth and looked like the inside of a sliced yam.
Just like the yam in Grandma's Saturday Soup.

祖母告訴我沙灘上的細沙好像新雪一樣，
但卻不會寒冷。

*Grandma tells me that the white powdery sand on the beaches looks like fresh snow but it's never cold.*

我能否用白沙造一個沙人呢？
那一定很有趣?!

I wonder if I could make a sandman with the white sand?
Wouldn't that be funny?!

星期三的雪下得更大，非常寒冷，
但我穿得很溫暖。
*當我去祖母的家時，她講有關牙買加的*
*故事給我聽。*

**Wednesday** the snow fell harder. It was cold but I was wrapped up warm.
*Grandma tells me stories about Jamaica when I go to her house.*

*「太陽每天照耀，令肌膚溫暖，*
*你只需要穿短褲和T-恤。」*
每天都和暖？短褲和T-恤？我真不能相信。

*"The sun shines every day. The sun is warm on your skin and you only need to wear your shorts and a T-shirt."*
Warm every day? Shorts and T-shirt? I can't believe that.

下午休息時，我們造雪球，互相拋擲。

At afternoon play we made snowballs
and threw them at each other.

The snowballs remind me of the round soft potatoes in Grandma's Saturday Soup.

那些雪球令我想起祖母的星期六湯的馬鈴薯。

星期四放學後，我和我的朋友莉娜跟她的
媽媽去圖書館。

On **Thursday** I went to the library after school with my friend Layla and her Mum.

我們路過公園時，看到兩個小球莖開始發芽，
嫩綠的苗芽在雪中凸出。
它們就好像祖母的星期六湯的青蔥。

As we passed the park we saw the little bulbs starting to grow. The little green shoots poked through the snow. They looked like the spring onions in Grandma's Saturday Soup.

*Grandma tells me about the wonderful plants and flowers in Jamaica.*
*"In Jamaica the most beautiful flowers grow wild.*
*They are all different colours and sizes*
*and their smell fills the air."*
I've never seen flowers like that before,
I wonder if she's only joking?

*祖母告訴我有關牙買加的奇妙植物和花卉。*
*「在牙買加，最漂亮的花是野生的，*
*它們有各種不同的顏色和大小，*
*空氣更充滿著它們的清香。」*
我從來未見過這樣的花，她是否在開玩笑呢？

星期五，爸爸和媽媽遲了上班。
「快，咪咪，挑一個水果，帶到學校去。」

On **Friday** Mum and Dad are late for work.
"Hurry Mimi, choose a piece of fruit to take to school."

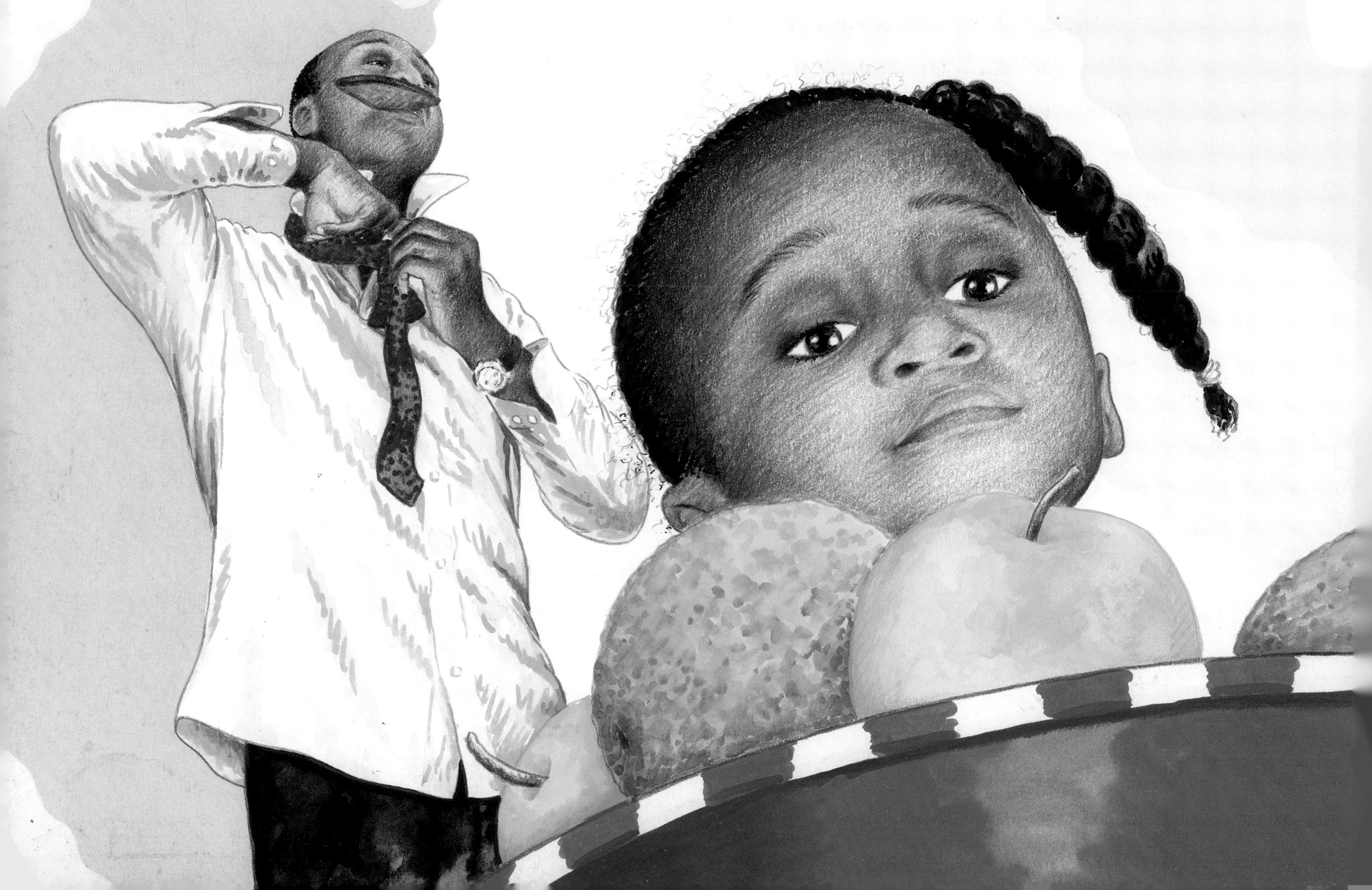

我看著果盤滿載的水果，
我應該挑選一個橙子、抑或一個蘋果、或者一個梨子呢？
蘋果和梨子的顏色和形狀令我想起祖母的星期六湯的佛手瓜。

I looked at the bowl full of fruit.
Should I choose an orange, an apple or a pear?
The apple and pear; their colour and shape remind me of the
cho-cho in Grandma's Saturday Soup.

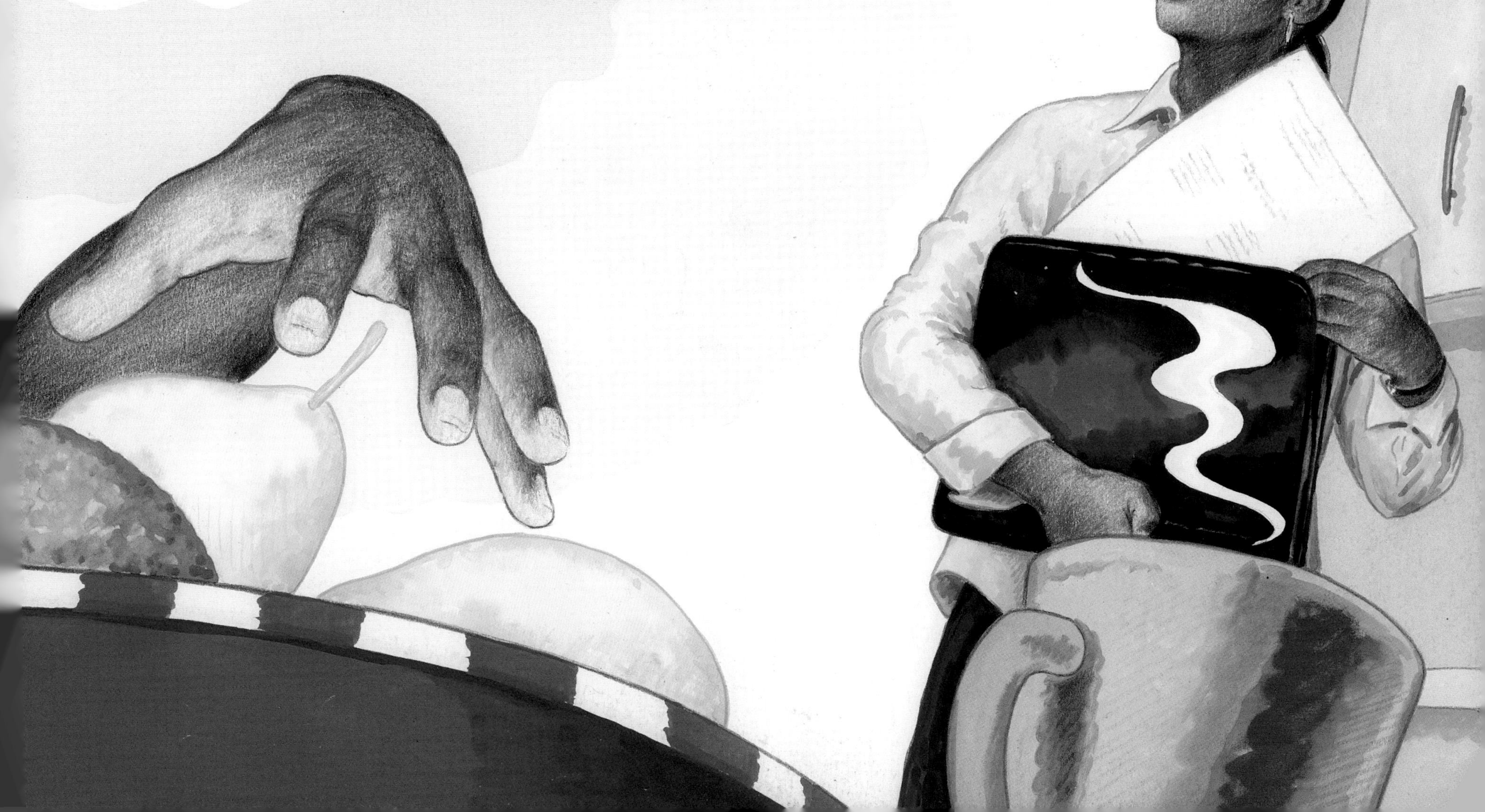

*祖母告訴我有關牙買加的水果。*
*「在牙買加，你可以走路上學，從樹上摘一個水果，*
*一個成熟的芒果，又多汁，又香甜。」*

*Grandma tells me about the fruits in Jamaica.*

*"In Jamaica you can walk to school and pick a piece of fruit from a tree, a ripe mango all juicy and sweet."*

放學後，為了獎勵我的好成績，媽媽帶我到電影院去。
當我們抵達時，太陽照耀著，但仍然是很寒冷，
我想春天很快便到了。

After school, as a treat for good marks, Mum and Dad took me to the cinema.
When we got there the sun was shining, but it was still cold.
I think springtime is coming.

電影很好看，當我們從電影院出來時，太陽已經開始落下了，
它又大又紅，就像祖母的星期六湯的大南瓜。

The film was great and when we came out the sun was setting over the town.
As it set it was big and orange just like the pumpkin in Grandma's Saturday Soup.

祖母告訴我有關牙買加的日出和日落。
「太陽很早便升起，令你感到清新，為新的一天作好準備。」

*Grandma tells me about the sunrise and sunsets in Jamaica.*
*"The sun rises early and makes you feel good and ready for your day."*

*「當太陽落下時，月亮便出現，跟著有百萬多顆星星像鑽石一樣在夜空中閃耀。」*

百萬顆星星，我實在不能想像有這麼多的星星。

*"When it sets and the moon comes out she is followed by a million stars that look like diamonds twinkling in the night sky."*

A million stars, I can't even imagine that many.

星期六早上，我去我的跳舞班。
音樂很慢和很幽怨。

**Saturday** morning I went to my dance class. The music was slow and sad.

*祖母告訴我有關即興小調和鋼鼓的節奏，有關人們在樹蔭下玩耍，一株長著像青蕉皮一樣的長樹葉的奇妙樹。*
*「那音樂令你開心快樂，感到想跟著音樂起舞。」*

*Grandma tells me about the rhythms of calypso music and steel drums, of people playing under the shade of a tree. A wonderful tree with long leaves that look like the strands of skin from a green banana.*
*"The music makes you happy and want to dance."*

媽媽開車來跳舞班接我。
我們沿著馬路駕駛，經過我的學校，在公園轉左，途經圖書館，
一直穿越鬧市，那裏有一間電影院，不會太遠了。

Mum picked me up after class. We went by car.
We drove down the road and past my school. We turned left at the park and on past the library. Through the town, there's the cinema and not much further now.

我很餓，實在很餓。我們終於來到祖母家。

I was hungry. Really hungry. At last we arrived at Grandma's.

我走向大門，已經聞到美味的氣味，
是青蕉、佛手瓜、甘薯、湯團、
馬鈴薯和大南瓜…

I ran to the front door and could smell a delicious smell. It's green bananas, cho-cho and yams, dumplings, potato, and pumpkin...

青蔥、雞、一大撮祖母的家鄉調味料和很多雞湯。
這就是祖母的星期六湯！

spring onions, chicken, a good pinch of Grandma's
country seasoning and a lot of chicken stock.
It's Grandma's Saturday Soup!

星期日，我們有朋友到家裏來吃飯，爸爸和媽媽都是廚藝能手，
但是在這個世界上，祖母的星期六湯是我最喜歡吃的食物。

On **Sunday** we had friends at our house for dinner.
Mum and Dad are good cooks, their food is nice but my favourite
food in the whole wide world is **Grandma's Saturday Soup**.